TITLE II-A

Awake and Dreaming

Awake and Dreaming

by Harve Zemach
pictures by Margot Zemach

Farrar, Straus & Giroux, New York

J
Z

Text and pictures copyright © 1970 by Farrar, Straus & Giroux, Inc.
All rights reserved
Library of Congress catalog card number: 77-125145 | SBN 374.3.0462.9
Printed in the United States of America
Published simultaneously in Canada by Doubleday Canada Ltd., Toronto
First edition, 1970

For Rebecca

There was once a young man who might have been happy had it not been for his dreams, which were so wild and strange and terrifying that a night's sleep left him more exhausted than a day's work. When he had tried all sorts of remedies with no success, he decided at last to take long walks in the countryside before bedtime, hoping to sleep more soundly afterward.

One evening as he walked he met an old woman gathering herbs in the twilight. He guessed from her appearance that she was a witch, and he begged her to tell him some secret to free him from his awful nightmares.

"Nightmares," she muttered, "I know everything about nightmares." She picked some wild poppies from the side of the road and handed them to the young man.

"Take these," she said. "Press them under your pillow. Tonight, if you see anything in your dream that you want, touch it and say, 'Come to me!' Then you will get rest . . . and something else besides."

That night the young man dreamed he was at a masked ball, or so it seemed. He was the only one not wearing a mask. The others ridiculed him and treated him cruelly. They milled about him, shrieked at him in hideous voices, and one of them struck at him repeatedly with a sword.

Remembering the witch's instructions, he suddenly caught hold of the sword and said, "Come to me!"

Instantly his dream vanished, and he slept peacefully the rest of the night. And in the morning, when he awoke, the sword lay by him, gleaming. The merchants of the city examined its blade, which was of finely worked silver, and its jewel-studded hilt, and told him it was of immense value and unlike any they had ever seen.

The next night he found himself (in a dream) standing on a broad grassy plain. Someone wrapped in a black cloak and riding a black horse was thundering across the plain toward him.

A moment later he felt himself bound by a thick rope, being dragged behind the horse and rider, bumping like a log over grass and stones.

He tried to cry out but was choked by the dust kicked up by the horse's hoofs. Desperate, he thrust a hand toward the sleek, handsome animal and gasped, "Come to me!"

Again the dream disappeared. And in the morning the magnificent horse stood firmly tethered in the courtyard beneath the young man's window.

On the third night he dreamed that he was in a cave full of treasure, and he was being tormented by wretched demons who threw fistfuls of gold and silver coins at him, crying: "Don't you want money? Here, have money!"

They threw more and more coins at him, and more and more, until he was covered with them, and still they threw more. He tried to dig his way out of the mountain of gold and silver pressing down on him, when suddenly remembering his power, he shouted, "Come to me!"

The dream ended, he slept peacefully, and in the morning he found piled up in his chamber an enormous treasure of gold and silver.

But on the same day there appeared at his door a stranger, an old man who said he was a messenger sent by the King of the Land of Dreams. "You have carried away my master's sword, his horse, and all his treasure," the messenger declared. "Now my master fears that you will rob him of other things. Therefore he proposes an agreement. If you swear you will carry away no more of his precious belongings, he promises to send you no more bad dreams."

"That is not enough!" cried the young man. "Your master, my enemy, has tortured me night after night for as long as I can remember. I demand that from now on he treat me especially kindly, as reward for all I have suffered. He must make my dreams as pleasant in the future as they have been terrible in the past!"

The messenger considered for a moment, and said: "It is agreed. Your dreams shall be as pleasant in the future as they have been terrible in the past. But if you should ever break your promise and take another thing away from the Land of Dreams, you shall again receive nightmares, twice as many and ten times more horrible than before."

After this the young man had only delightful dreams, from which he awakened cheerful and refreshed. He once dreamed that he lay in a field of fragrant wildflowers, while all around him gorgeous butterflies, such as he had never seen in his waking hours, flitted from blossom to blossom. Another time he found himself high in the branches of a cherry tree; and the cherries tasted so sweet and delicious that he sighed in his sleep and murmured, "Ah, if only I had such a tree in my garden."

But as tempting as it seemed at times to reach out and touch the wonders that filled his dreams, and no matter how he might yearn to bring something back with him out of sleep and keep it with him always, he could not forget his promise or the suffering he had endured before. And so he let himself be satisfied with dreaming.

Until one night he met in a dream a lady who was most enchantingly beautiful. Night after night she appeared to him, only to vanish again each time he awoke. He walked with her through forests and by the side of streams. They talked about many things, and in one of his dreams he told her that he loved her more than the sun and the stars.

Repeatedly he caught himself reaching out to touch her and say "Come to me!"—that he might bring her away from the Land of Dreams and make her his wife. But each time he stopped himself, for he knew he could not bear to live with the terrible visions and nightmares that would afterward pursue him.

And so his pleasant and delightful dreams came to trouble and pain him. The more he dreamed of the beautiful lady, the more he longed to have her. Now again he awoke each morning trembling and exhausted, no longer from nightmares but from the night-long struggle to keep himself from breaking his agreement with the King of the Land of Dreams.

At last one evening, full of despair and counting himself the most unlucky man in the world, he returned to the place where he had met the witch. She appeared, and again he begged her for help.

"Do you love the beautiful lady more than the sun and the stars?" asked the witch.

"Yes, I do," he replied.

"Then, if you want her to be yours forever," said she, "you yourself must become a dream."

"How can I become a dream?" he asked.

The witch gave him a tiny bottle filled with an inky potion. "Take this home," she said. "Drink it tonight."

That night the young man drank the potion, fell asleep, and dreamed a dream which never ended. He and the beautiful lady lived happily together in the Land of Dreams, and they do to this day. They live in a palace. In their garden stands a cherry tree, and nearby is a field of wildflowers where butterflies flutter from blossom to blossom.

Printed by Neff Lithographing Company, New York City
Bound by H. Wolff Book Manufacturing Company, New York City
Typography by Atha Tehon

89404

DATE DUE